THE ALFIE
TREASURY

Shirley Hughes

TED SMART

A TED SMART Publication 1996

This edition first published in 1994 by
The Bodley Head Children's Books
An imprint of Random House UK Ltd
20 Vauxhall Bridge Road
London SW1V 2SA

Alfie Gets in First © Shirley Hughes 1981
Alfie's Feet © Shirley Hughes 1982
Alfie Gives a Hand © Shirley Hughes 1983
An Evening at Alfie's © Shirley Hughes 1984

Shirley Hughes has asserted her right under the Copyright,
Designs and Patents Act 1988 to be identified as the author of
this work

Printed in Hong Kong

A catalogue record for this book is available
from the British Library

ISBN 0 09 180443 4

CONTENTS

ALFIE GETS IN FIRST

One day Alfie and Mum and Annie Rose were coming home from the shops. Alfie ran on ahead because he wanted to get home first. He ran all the way from the corner to the front gate and up the steps to the front door.

Then he sat down on the top step and
waited for the others. Along came Mum,
pushing Annie Rose and the shopping.

"I raced you!" called Alfie. "I'm back
first, so there!"

Annie Rose didn't care. She was tired.
She sat back in her push-chair and sucked
her thumb.

10

Mum put the brake on the push-chair and
left Annie Rose at the bottom of the steps
while she lifted the basket of shopping up to
the top. Then she found the key and opened
the front door. Alfie dashed in ahead of her.

"I've won, I've won!" he shouted.

Mum put the shopping down in the hall and
went back down the steps to lift Annie Rose
out of her push-chair. But what do you think
Alfie did then?

He gave the door a great big slam – BANG!
– just like that.

Then Mum was outside the door, holding
Annie Rose, and Alfie was inside with the
shopping. Mum's key was inside too.

"Open the door, Alfie," said Mum.

But Alfie didn't know how to open the door from the inside. The catch was too high up. Mum looked into the letter-box.

"Try to reach the catch and turn it," she said. Alfie tried but he couldn't quite reach it.

"Can you put the key through the letter-box?" said Mum. But Alfie couldn't reach the letter-box either.

Annie Rose was hungry as well as tired. She began to cry. Then Alfie began to cry too. He didn't like being all by himself on the wrong side of the door. Just then Mrs MacNally came hurrying across the street to see what all the noise was about.

She and Mum took it in turns to say
encouraging things into the letter-box.
But Alfie still couldn't open the door.

"Go and fetch your little chair from the sitting-room and then you'll be able to reach the catch," said Mum. But Alfie didn't try to fetch his little chair. He just went on crying, louder and louder, and Annie Rose cried louder and louder too.

"There's my Maureen," said Mrs MacNally. "I'm sure she'll be able to help."

Mrs MacNally's Maureen was a big girl. Right away she came and joined Mum and Annie Rose and Mrs MacNally on the top step.

"Mmm, might have to break a window," she said. "But I'll try to climb up the drain-pipe first, if you like."

But Mrs MacNally didn't like that idea at all.

"Oh no, Maureen, you might hurt yourself," she said.

Just then Alfie's very good friend the milkman came up the street in his milk-float.

When he saw Mum and Annie Rose and Mrs MacNally
and Mrs MacNally's Maureen all standing on the top
step he stopped his float and said:
"What's the trouble?"
So they told him.
"Don't worry, mate," the milkman shouted. "We'll
soon have you out of there."

"Mmm, looks as though this lock's going to be difficult to break," said the milkman. But then Mrs MacNally's Maureen had a very good idea. She ran to ask the window-cleaner, who was working up the street, if he would bring his ladder and climb up to the bathroom window. And, of course, when the window-cleaner heard about Alfie he came hurrying along with his ladder as quickly as he could.

Then Mum and Annie Rose and Mrs MacNally and Mrs MacNally's Maureen and the milkman all stood on the top step and watched while the window-cleaner put his ladder up against the house. He started to climb up to the bathroom window. But when he was half-way up the ladder, what do you think happened?

The front door suddenly opened and there
was Alfie! He had managed to reach the catch
and turn it – like that – after all.

He was *very* pleased with himself.
He opened the front door
as wide as it would go and
stood back grandly to let
everybody in.

Then the window-cleaner came down from his ladder, and he and the milkman and Mrs MacNally's Maureen and Mrs MacNally and Annie Rose and Mum and Alfie all went into the kitchen and had tea together.

ALFIE'S FEET

This little pig went to market,

This little pig stayed at home,

This little pig had roast beef,

This little pig had none,

And this little pig cried, Wee-wee-wee-wee-wee,

I can't find my way home.

Alfie had a little sister called Annie Rose.
Alfie's feet were quite big. Annie Rose's feet
were rather small. They were all soft and pink
underneath. Alfie knew a game he could play
with Annie Rose, counting her toes.

Annie Rose had lots of different ways of getting about. She went forwards, crawling,

and backwards, on her behind,

and she liked to slide
about very fast on her potty,

skidding round and round
on the floor and in and out
of the table legs.

Annie Rose had
some new red shoes.

She could walk in them
a bit, if she was pushing her
little cart or holding on to
someone's hand.

When they went out, Annie Rose wore her
red shoes and Alfie wore his old brown ones.
Mum usually helped him put them on, because
he wasn't very good at doing up the laces yet.

If it had been raining Alfie
liked to go stamping about in
mud and walking through puddles,

splish, splash, SPLOSH!

Then his shoes got rather wet.

So did his socks,

and so did his feet.

So one Saturday morning Alfie and Mum went to
a big shop in the High Street.

48

They bought a pair of shiny new yellow boots
for Alfie to wear when he went stamping about
in mud and walking through puddles. Alfie was
very pleased. He carried them home himself in a
cardboard box.

When they got in, Alfie sat down at
once and unwrapped his new boots. He
put them on all by himself and walked
about in them,

stamp! stamp! stamp!

He went into the kitchen to show Mum and Dad
and Annie Rose, stamping his feet all the way,

stamp! stamp! stamp!

The boots were very smart
and shiny but they felt funny.

Alfie wanted to go out again right away. So he put on his mac, and Dad took his book and his newspaper and they went off to the park.

Alfie stamped in a lot of mud and walked through a lot of puddles, splish, splash, SPLOSH! He frightened some sparrows who were having a bath. He even frightened two big ducks. They went hurrying back to their pond, walking with their feet turned in.

Alfie looked down at his feet. They still
felt funny. They kept turning outwards.
Dad was sitting on a bench. They both
looked at Alfie's feet.

Suddenly Alfie knew what was wrong!

Dad lifted Alfie on to the bench beside him and helped him to take off each boot and put it on the other foot. And when Alfie stood down again his feet didn't feel a bit funny any more.

After tea Mum painted a big black R on to one of Alfie's boots and a big black L on the other to help Alfie remember which boot was which. The R was for Right foot and the L was for Left foot. The black paint wore off in the end and the boots stopped being new and shiny, but Alfie usually did remember to get them on the proper way round after that. They felt much better when he went stamping about in mud and walking through puddles.

And, of course, Annie Rose made such a fuss about Alfie having new boots that she had to have a pair of her own to go stamping about in too, splish, splash, SPLOSH!

ALFIE
GIVES A HAND

One day Alfie came home from Nursery School with a card in an envelope. His best friend, Bernard, had given it to him.

"Look, it's got my name on it," said
Alfie, pointing.

Mum said that it was an invitation to
Bernard's birthday tea party.

"Will it be at Bernard's house?" Alfie wanted to know. He'd never been there before. Mum said yes, and she told him all about birthday parties, and how you had to take a present, and about the games and how there would be nice things to eat.

Alfie was very excited about Bernard's party. When the day came Mum washed Alfie's face and brushed his hair and helped him put on a clean T-shirt and his brand-new shorts.

"You and Annie Rose are going to be at the party, too, aren't you?" asked Alfie.

"Oh, no," said Mum. "I'll take you to Bernard's house and then Annie Rose and I will go to the park and come back to collect you when it's time to go home."

"But I want you to be there," said Alfie.

Mum told him that she and Annie Rose hadn't been invited to the party, only Alfie, because he was Bernard's special friend.

"You don't mind my leaving you at Nursery School, do you?" she said. "So you won't mind being at Bernard's house either, as soon as you get there."

Mum had bought some crayons for Alfie to give Bernard for his birthday present. While she was wrapping them up, Alfie went upstairs. He looked under his pillow and found his old bit of blanket which he kept in bed with him at night.

He brought it downstairs, and sat down to wait for Mum.

"You won't want your old blanket
at the party," said Mum, when
it was time to go.

But Alfie wouldn't leave
his blanket behind. He held
it tightly with one hand,
and Bernard's present with
the other, all the way to
Bernard's house.

When they got there, Bernard's Mum opened the door.
"Hello, Alfie," she said. "Let's go into the garden
and find Bernard and the others."
Then Mum gave Alfie a kiss and said good-bye,
and went off to the park with Annie Rose.

"Would you like to put your blanket down here with the coats?" asked Bernard's Mum. But Alfie didn't want to put his blanket down. He still held on to it very tightly.

Bernard was in the garden with Min and Sam and Daniel and some other children from the Nursery School.

"Happy birthday!" Alfie remembered to say, and he gave Bernard his present. Bernard pulled off the paper.

"Crayons! How lovely!" said Bernard's Mum. "Say thank you, Bernard."
"Thank you," said Bernard. But do you know what he did then?

He threw the crayons up in the air. They landed all
over the grass.

"That was a silly thing to do," said Bernard's Mum,
as she picked up the crayons and put them away.

Then Bernard's Mum brought out some bubble stuff
and blew lots of bubbles into the air. They floated all
over the garden and the children jumped about trying
to pop them.

Alfie couldn't pop many bubbles because he was holding
on to his blanket. But Bernard jumped about and pushed
and popped more bubbles than anyone else.

"Don't push people, Bernard," said Bernard's Mum sternly.

One huge bubble landed
lightly on Min's sleeve. It
stayed there, quivering and
shiny. Min smiled. She
stood very still.

Then Bernard came up
behind her and popped
the big bubble.

Min began to cry.
Bernard's Mum was
cross with Bernard and
told him to say he
was sorry.

"Never mind, we're going to have tea now, dear," she told
Min. "Who would you like to sit next to?"

Min wanted to sit next to Alfie. She stopped crying and
pulled her chair right up close to his.

For tea there were sandwiches and little sausages on sticks and crisps and jellies and a big iced cake with candles and "Happy Birthday, Bernard" written on it.

Bernard took a huge breath and blew out
all the candles at once – *Phoooooo!* Everyone
clapped and sang "Happy Birthday to You".

Then Bernard blew into his lemonade through his straw and made rude bubbling noises. He blew into his jelly, too, until his Mum took it away from him.

Alfie liked the tea . . . but holding on to his blanket made eating rather difficult. It got all mixed up with the jelly and crisps, and covered in sticky crumbs.

After tea, Bernard's Mum said that they were all going to play a game. But Bernard ran off and fetched his very best present. It was a tiger mask.

Bernard went behind a bush and came out wearing the mask and making terrible growling noises: "Grrr! Grrr, grrrr, GRRRR! ACHT!"

He went crawling round the garden, sounding very fierce and frightening.

Min began to cry again. She clung on to Alfie.

"Get up *at once*, Bernard," said Bernard's Mum. "It's not that kind of game. Now let's all stand in a circle, everyone, and join hands."

Bernard stopped growling, but he wouldn't take off his tiger mask. Instead he grabbed Alfie's hand to pull him into the circle.

Bernard's Mum tried to take Min's hand and bring her into the circle, too. But Min wouldn't hold anyone's hand but Alfie's. She went on crying. She cried and cried.

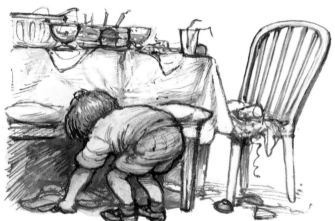

Then Alfie made a brave decision. He ran and put down his blanket, very carefully, in a safe place underneath the table.

Now he could hold Min's hand, too, as well as Bernard's.

Min stopped crying. She wasn't
frightened of Bernard in his tiger mask
now she was holding Alfie's hand.

She joined in the game and they all danced round together, singing:

"Ring-a-ring-o'-roses
A pocket full of posies
A-tishoo, a-tishoo,
We all fall DOWN!"

Afterwards Alfie and Min joined in with some more games and ate ice-cream and pop-corn and bounced balloons with the others. Alfie had such a good time that his blanket stayed under the table until Mum and Annie Rose came to collect him.

"What a helpful guest you've been, Alfie," said Bernard's Mum, when Alfie thanked her and said good-bye. "Min wouldn't have enjoyed the party a bit without you. I *do* wish Bernard would learn to be helpful sometimes –

– Perhaps he will, one day."

On the way home, Alfie carried his blanket in one hand and a balloon and a packet of sweets in the other. His blanket had got a bit messy at the party. It had been rather in the way, too. Next time he thought he might leave it safely at home, after all.

AN EVENING
AT ALFIE'S

One cold, winter evening . . .

Alfie and his little sister, Annie Rose, were
all ready for bed,

Mum and Dad were all ready to go out,

and Mrs MacNally's Maureen was in the living-room.
She had come to look after Alfie and Annie Rose
while Mum and Dad went to a party.

Alfie and Maureen waved good-bye to them from the window.

Annie Rose was already in her cot. Soon she settled down and went to sleep.

Alfie liked Maureen. She always read him a
story when she came to baby-sit.

Tonight Alfie wanted the story about Noah and his Ark full of animals. Alfie liked to hear how the rain came drip, drip, drip, and then splash! splash! splash! and then rushing everywhere, until the whole world was covered with water.

When Maureen had finished the story it was time for Alfie to go to bed. She came upstairs to tuck him up. They had to be very quiet and talk in whispers in case they woke up Annie Rose.

Maureen gave Alfie a good-night hug and went off downstairs, leaving the door a little bit open.

Alfie didn't feel sleepy. He lay in bed
looking at the patch of light on the ceiling. For
a long time all was quiet. Then he heard a
funny noise outside on the landing.

Alfie sat up. The noise was just outside his door. Drip, drip, drip! Soon it got quicker. It changed to drip-drip, drip-drip, drip-drip! It was getting louder too.

Alfie got out of bed and peeped round the door. There was a puddle on the floor. He looked up. Water was splashing into the puddle from the ceiling, drip-drip, drip-drip, drip-drip! It was raining inside the house!

Alfie went downstairs. Maureen was doing
her homework in front of the television.
"It's raining on the landing," Alfie told her.

Alfie and Maureen went back upstairs. The
puddle was getting bigger. The drip-drip,
drip-drip, drip-drip had turned into a splash!
splash! splash!

"Hmm, looks like a burst pipe," said Maureen. A plumber was one of the things she wanted to be when she left school.

"Better get a bucket," she said. So Alfie showed her where the bucket was kept, in the kitchen cupboard with the brushes and brooms.

But now the water was
dripping down in another
place. Alfie and Maureen
found two of Mum's big
mixing bowls and put them
underneath the drips.

Maureen got on the telephone to her Mum. The MacNallys lived just across the street. Mrs MacNally was there in a moment.

"Oh dear, oh dear, it's ruining your mother's floor!" cried Mrs MacNally. "Fetch some floor-cloths, Maureen!"

Just then Annie Rose woke up and began to cry.
"Shh, shh, there, there," said Mrs MacNally,
bending over her cot. But Annie Rose
only looked at her and cried louder.

Mrs MacNally ran back out to the landing. She and Maureen tried to mop up the water. But now the drips were coming from lots of different places, splash, splash, splash!

"We ought to turn the water off from the main," said Maureen, "but I don't know how you do it. I think I'd better fetch Dad."

While she was gone Mrs MacNally mopped
and mopped, and emptied brimming bowls,
and in between mopping and emptying she ran
to try to comfort Annie Rose. But Annie Rose
went on crying and crying. The drips on the
landing came faster and faster.

Now there were a lot of puddles on the floor. Alfie paddled in them for a while. It was quite fun but the water was very cold. He thought that soon perhaps the whole street would be covered with water and they would all have to float away in a boat, like Noah's Ark.

Soon Maureen came running
upstairs with Mr MacNally close
behind her, wearing his bedroom
slippers.

"What's all this, then?" said Mr
MacNally, looking at all the water
pouring down.

He put his head round the bedroom door. He and Annie Rose were old friends.

"Dear, dear, what's all this?" he said in a very kind voice.

Then he went downstairs and found a large sort of tap under the stairs and turned it off, just like that.

"So *that's* where it was," said Maureen.

Then the water stopped pouring down
through the ceiling, splash! splash! splash! and
became a drip-drip, drip-drip, drip-drip,

and then a drip. . . drip. . . . drip. . . . . drip. . . . . .
and then it stopped altogether.

"Oh, thank goodness for
that!" said Mrs MacNally.

"I'll know how to do it
next time," said Maureen.

But Annie Rose was still crying.

Alfie went into the bedroom to see if he could cheer her up. Tears were rolling down her cheeks and soaking into her blanket.

"Don't cry, Annie Rose," said Alfie. And he put his hand through the bars of her cot and patted her very gently, as he had seen Mum do sometimes.

Annie Rose still wore nappies at night.

"Annie Rose is wet," Alfie told everyone. "And her bed's wet too. I expect that's why she's crying."

"Why, so she is, poor little mite!" said Mrs MacNally.

When Annie Rose was all dry and comfortable again, Mrs MacNally put her on the living-room sofa with Alfie and tucked a quilt round them. Then she gave them both a biscuit.

Annie Rose was quite cheerful now.
She got very friendly with Mr MacNally
and he let her play a game with him,
taking off his glasses and putting
them on again. Then she sucked her
thumb and leaned up against Alfie,
and Alfie leaned up against her. When
Mum and Dad came home, they were
both fast asleep.

Next morning Mum told Alfie not to turn on the taps until the plumber had been to mend the burst pipe.

Alfie didn't mind not having a wash. He'd had enough water the evening before to last for a long time.